Dory

Nemo

Ward

Sheldon

Pearl

Published by Hachette Partworks Ltd.
ISBN: 978-1-906965-66-2
Date of Printing: December 2011
Printed in Singapore by Tien Wah Press

DISNEY · PIXAR

FINDING NEMO

BRUCE BREAKS LOOSE!

DISNEY · PIXAR
hachette

WOW! I was so happy – I was going on my very first camping trip! There were so many fish in the class that my dad, Marlin, asked his special friend Dory to come along and lend a fin.

Dory's a bit of a flake, with a terrible memory. But she loves to watch out for others – if you're in a spot, you can always count on Dory.

Before we left, my pink friend Pearl turned to me. "Will it be OK, Nemo? Really?"

"Don't you worry," I said. "If there's one fish who'll keep you safe, it's Dad!"

"Yeah," snarled tough guy Ward. "Nemo never leaves home without his baby-sitter!"

"You can talk, Ward," said Tad. "You get scared every time we have a sleep-over!"

Then Dory appeared. "Hi, Nono!" she said. "I mean, Nemo! And all you other guys, too. Sorry, I have trouble with names. Shall we get going?" She smiled and waved her flipper.

Suddenly Bruce, the great white shark, cruised up alongside us. "Hello!" he barked.

"Yikes!" cried the class. Everyone always gets a shock when that huge, toothy shark appears.

"Sorry, guys," he said. "I was just passing by and I thought I'd say hi."

"I don't want to die!" squeaked Ward. He streaked off to hide behind Pearl.

"Chill out, guys," I said. "Bruce won't eat you!"

Dory joined in. "Sure, I know him. Mr Big Tooth Shark. You're my friend, aren't you?"

"Yes, I've learnt my lesson," said Bruce. "Fish are my friends. I don't eat them any more."

So there was nothing to fear. Almost certainly.

Bruce turned to my dad. "How you doing, Marlin? You look busy!"

"I'm taking the kids camping," Dad replied, nervously.

"Camping?" exclaimed Bruce, in a shaky voice. "I think I'm gonna cry. My dad never took me camping. You're so lucky, Nemo."

Dad told us we had to learn all about the dangers of the sea bed. "See that plant?" he said. "Don't go near it. Ever. If you touch it, you'll get a terrible... oh! *AAAAAAAH!*"

He pulled a funny face and started scratching furiously. Hmmm. Maybe he got a bit too close?

"Yow! Oooch!" he yelped. "That itches!"

"This needs treatment," muttered Dad. "Sorry, kids, we'll have to go home."

Oh no! No camping trip!

"Hold on, Marlin," said Dory. "The kids could still go camping with me and Bruce. How about it, kids?"

"Oh, yeah!" we all cried.

Dad nodded. "Well, OK," he said, reluctantly.

"But you have to be very, very careful. If you see any big fish, you must go and hide behind Bruce's fins. Is that clear?"

Then he headed off home, to get his itch seen to.

"That's a fine dad you've got there, Nemo," said
Bruce. "He's always looking out for you. I never even
knew my father!"

"Poor Bruce," said Dory, kindly.

"But hey," I added. "Today, you're going camping!
And you get a chance to do something your father
didn't – take care of someone!"

"True," said Bruce. "Better late than never!"

"I'm really going to do my best," promised Bruce. "I'll look after all of you, just like Dory does."

"Huh?" said Dory. "What are we talking about here?"

"Don't you remember?" I asked. "You're taking us camping, with Bruce! We're gonna have fun!"

"Oh yeah, I remember now. So here we go!" She thought for a moment. "But... where?"

Bruce smiled. "I know a quiet spot not so far from here," he suggested.

"Cool!" cried all the kids, except one.

"No way!" yelled Ward. "Go camping with a shark? You must be joking! Do I have to spell it out for you? Sharks... eat... fish!"

"I'm not scared," I said. "I trust Bruce. He's our friend!" I knew that Ward wanted to come really. He wouldn't want to look like a wimp.

Eventually he agreed to
come, but he wasn't happy
about it. "We'll be sorry!" he
predicted. So off we swam
with Bruce. "Where are you
taking us?" I asked him.

"You and your friends – you want to have some
fun, right?" he asked, giving me a wicked grin.

Sheldon the seahorse whispered in my ear. "Ward says the shark is gonna eat us!"

"He won't do that," I said. "Bruce has been off the fish for a long time now."

"Here we are, folks!" roared Bruce, proudly. "When I was knee-high to a flatfish, I loved to hang out here." He pointed to the wreck of a pirate ship!

I was a little scared, but mostly I felt excited. I couldn't wait to get inside and explore!

"I don't like it," muttered Sheldon.

"C'mon, guys," I declared, fighting back a tremble in my voice. "If Bruce says it's safe, you can bet we'll have fun. We might even find some pirate treasure!"

"Perfect!" gasped Dory. "Let's find a place to pitch camp."

"And I'll get something to eat," added Bruce.

Everyone was delighted, except Ward. He liked to seem tough, but it was all an act.

I went with Sheldon to explore the ship. "Seen
Pearl?" he asked.

"Uh, no. Not lately," I said. "I think she's gone
looking for shells, with Tad."

"What are you two yapping about?" said Ward,
poking his nose in as usual.

"We can't find Pearl and Tad," said Sheldon.

"Hey," said Ward. "That's funny. I can't see Bruce!
That shark is gonna eat us, one by one!"

"Bruce isn't like that, Ward," I argued. "He's a
changed shark."

"Let's look for Pearl and Tad," exclaimed Dory.

"Good idea," I said. "Let's go."

Ward shot off ahead of us. When I got to the sunken ship, I found him with Bruce.

"Hi, Ward," said Bruce, politely.

Ward shivered in terror.

"Come here, Bruce," he quavered. "I've got something to show you."

What was Ward up to?

Ward backed off slyly, pointing at a
rusty cage. "Bruce," said Ward, "I think
a fish has got caught in this cage."

"Really?" asked Bruce. "Do you think
he's stuck?

"See for yourself!" said Ward.

Bruce poked his head into the cage.

"He's at the other end," said Ward,
looking at the piece of metal that
propped open the door.

"I'm gonna help!" said Bruce, going
further in.

Ward grabbed the
piece of metal and
pulled with all his
might. But it was
stuck fast!
"Watch out, Bruce!"
I yelled.

Bruce heard my warning and started to turn, but all
he managed was to knock the door shut. CLANG!
"I caught my first shark!" said Ward, proudly.

"No, dummy!" I said. "You've caught my friend!"
"Take it easy, people!" said Bruce, calmly. "What's
    the problem here?"

"Your problem,
Bruce, is that
you're trapped!"
chuckled Ward.
He sounded smug, but he
stayed well clear of the bars!

"It's OK, Bruce," I said. "I'll
get you out of there."

But I couldn't. I just
couldn't open that door!

"I'll get Dory," I said. "She'll know what to do."
And I swam off to find our forgetful guardian.

I was heading away from the ship when
suddenly I found I was surrounded by moray
eels! I tried to turn and get away, but they
came after me. They looked very fierce and
very hungry!

A voice came out of nowhere. "Coco! I mean,
Neeeemo!" It couldn't be anyone but Dory.
But where was she hiding?

Dory poked her head out of a crack in the ship's hull. "Hi!" she yelled. "Wanna see the camp site?"

I rushed for Dory and she dragged me through the crack. But there was an eel right on my tail!

BONK! The ship rattled as the eel banged his head on the hull. He couldn't fit through the gap!

The whole class was hiding inside the wreck. Even Ward was there, keeping clear of those evil eels!

"Well done, Nemo!" cried Pearl. "But we aren't safe yet."

"We can fight off the eels," I said, "but only if Bruce helps us. And stupid Ward locked him up in a cage!"

"My first shark!" said Ward, still very pleased with himself.

Everyone shouted, "Shut up, Ward!"

"C'mon, Nemo," gasped Dory. "I'll help you. We've got to set Bruce free."

It was the only way to get the better of those slippery meanies!

With Dory, I sneaked out into the open. Luckily, the eels didn't spot us.

We hid under some seaweed. "Not a sound, Dory," I warned. "These eels are extremely dangerous and they look hungry!"

"Sure thing," she answered. "And once we find, uh... who are we looking for, again?"

"Bruce!" I yelled. "The shark!"

"We're looking for a shark?" Dory asked, puzzled. "Is that a good idea?"

"He's a nice shark," I said. "He can save us from the eels!"

Dory didn't remember anything at all. This was going to be difficult!

We reached the cage. "Dory! Nemo!" said Bruce. "Am I glad to see you!"

"We need your help, Bruce," I said. "We're stuck below decks, and we're under attack by eels!"

"They're so nasty!" explained Dory.

"No problem, guys," growled Bruce. "I can sort them out, if you can set me free."

We all leaned hard on the door, but it wouldn't budge. Then I had an idea.

I remembered what Bruce had said to us.
He wanted to take care of us like a father.
And I knew that when my dad was looking
out for me, he could get very, very strong!

I just had to jog Bruce's memory.

"Think of the kids, Bruce!" I yelled. "If you don't get free, the moray eels will eat them!"

Bruce frowned. "*Moray* eels? I hate those critters! They go after little fish who can't defend themselves. When I was a sharklet, they used to pick on me!" He was getting angrier and angrier. "I had no one to protect me. But you kids... you've got BRUCE to look after you!"

"*GRRRAAAAAAAAAAAAAAH!*"
Bruce snapped the bars of his cage!
"Show me where your friends are! I'll save them!" he roared.
"Uh... Hoho," said Dory. "Show him!"

"Follow me!" I said.
    We swam around the ship and found the eels getting ready to attack. But Bruce got their attention, super quick!
    "Never fear, BRUCE is here!" he growled.

In a flash, the eels were gone.

The class came out of hiding to thank Bruce. We all cheered – well, all except Ward. He looked pretty sheepish, and stayed out of the celebrations.

"Hey, guys!" said Bruce. "I know a great place to camp! Wanna go?"

"Yeah! *YEAHHHHH!*" we shouted.

Bruce took us to the place that my dad had planned to visit – a beautiful, colourful coral reef!

Later, Ward came up to Bruce. "I thought it would be a big deal to catch a shark," he said. "But I was stupid."

"It's OK," said Bruce. "I'm not as mean as I look. In fact, I reckon I'd make a pretty cool dad – what d'you think?"

Ward thought for a moment. "Er... maybe," he muttered. Everyone laughed, and Bruce laughed loudest of all!